THE JEWEL SMU[ ]

Peyo

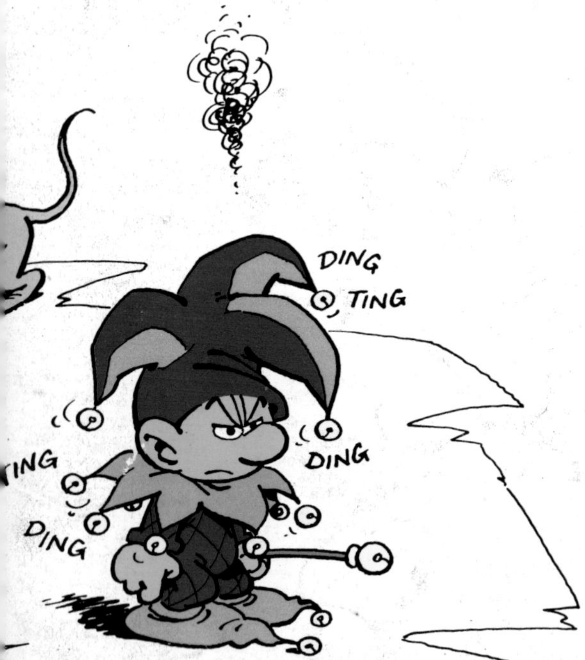

DING
TING
DING
TING
DING

THE JEWEL SMURFER

A **SMURFS** GRAPHIC NOVEL BY *Peyo*

WITH THE COLLABORATION OF
LUC PARTHOENS AND THIERRY CULLIFORD FOR THE SCRIPT,
ALAIN MAURY AND LUC PARTHOENS FOR ARTWORK,
NINE AND STUDIO LÉONARDO FOR COLORS.

PAPERCUTZ™
NEW YORK

SMURFS GRAPHIC NOVELS AVAILABLE FROM **PAPERCUTZ**™

THE SMURFS graphic novels are available in paperback for $5.99 each and in hardcover for $10.99 each at booksellers everywhere. You can also order online at papercutz.com. Or call 1-800-886-1223, Monday through Friday, 9 – 5 EST. MC, Visa, and AmEx accepted. To order by mail, please add $4.00 for postage and handling for first book ordered, $1.00 for each additional book and make check payable to NBM Publishing. Send to: Papercutz, 160 Broadway, Suite 700, East Wing, New York, NY 10038.

THE SMURFS graphic novels are also available digitally wherever e-books are sold.

PAPERCUTZ.COM

 THE JEWEL SMURFER

"The Jewel Smurfer"
BY PEYO
WITH THE COLLABORATION OF
LUC PARTHOENS AND THIERRY CULLIFORD FOR THE SCRIPT,
ALAIN MAURY AND LUC PARTHOENS FOR ARTWORK,
NINE AND STUDIO LÉONARDO FOR COLORS.

Joe Johnson, *SMURFLATIONS*
Adam Grano, *SMURFIC DESIGN*
Janice Chiang, *LETTERING SMURFETTE*
Matt. Murray, *SMURF CONSULTANT*
Jeff Whitman, *SMURF COORDINATOR*
Bethany Bryan, *ASSOCIATE SMURFETTE*
Jim Salicrup, *SMURF-IN-CHIEF*

PAPERBACK EDITION ISBN: 978-1-62991-194-6
HARDCOVER EDITION ISBN: 978-1-62991-195-3

PRINTED IN CHINA AUGUST 2015 BY WKT CO. LTD.
3/F PHASE 1 LEADER INDUSTRIAL CENTRE
188 TEXACO ROAD, TSEUN WAN, N.T., HONG KONG

Papercutz books may be purchased for business or promotional use. For information on bulk purchases please contact Macmillan Corporate and Premium Sales Department at (800) 221-7945 x5442.

DISTRIBUTED BY MACMILLAN
FIRST PAPERCUTZ PRINTING

THE JEWEL SMURFER

The Smurfs Village has been astir for the past few days. They're getting ready, it turns out, for the great festival of the spring equinox...

Chef Smurf and Greedy Smurf are preparing the buffet...

Hefty Smurf and Smurfette are practicing their roles as Romeo and Smurfiette...

Handy Smurf and Dopey Smurf are seeing to the decorations...

As for Papa Smurf, he makes sure everybody accomplishes his task...

Vanity Smurf, have you seen Brainy Smurf or Jokey Smurf?

Not since you smurfed them to the forest, Papa Smurf!

What could those two still be smurfing? I don't like them being that far from the village for so long!

© Peyo

1

Somewhere in the forest...

Why is it always us that Papa Smurf chooses to send to the forest to smurf something for him?

It gets really smurfing after a while!

If you hadn't made a gift smurf up in my face right when Papa Smurf was looking for volunteers, maybe he wouldn't have chosen us...

And also, when Papa Smurf says something, we have to smurf it, because he's Papa Smurf and we must always smurf what Papa Smurf says...

In any case, we're here.

The Ford of the Merry Smurfer! It's the only place where you can smurf the cattail stems Papa Smurf asked us to get!

Well, what are we smurfing on? Let's go!

Uh... wait for me, Jokey Smurf!

Maybe we should smurf more carefully! Remember, Papa Smurf told us that humans sometimes smurfed here!

For smurf's sake, that's right! Look out, Brainy Smurf! **HUMANS!**

SPLOOSH

I'll tell Papa Smurf about this, Jokey Smurf... And you'll be severely smurfed!

HEE HEE HEE!

HEE HEE HEE!
You're so smurfy, Brainy Smurf!

HEE HEE! OOPS!

BONK

Heh heh! You got a taste of your own medismurf! Didn't you, Jokey Smurf?

SPLASH

Okay, that's enough now! You're not making anybody laugh with your smurferies! Come out of the water!...

For smurf's sake! He knocked himself out smurfing on the rock! Jokey Smurf, wake up!

At that instant...

We're not very far now from the town of Abélagot!

CREECREECREECREE

3

7

CREEE CREEECREEE

Oh, smurf! Humans!

CREEE CREEE

→OOF!←... He's too heavy! I... →huff← ... I won't be able to smurf him.... →puff← ... Into the bushes... →Hmpff.←

What-- What should I smurf?

P-- PAPA SMURF!

Really, Godillot, I don't know what you see in that stupid mouse! It's not at all getting the tricks we're trying to teach it!

That's because it feels intimidated when people look at it!

HEY LOOK! Adhémar! THERE! On the road!

What is it?

?

?!

It looks like an elf! You see how little it is?

Can I keep it, Adhémar?

Sure! But let's not linger here! If there's one elf, there may be others!... And I don't like that!

It's a catasmurfe! I absolutely must tell Papa Smurf!

© Peyo

4

8

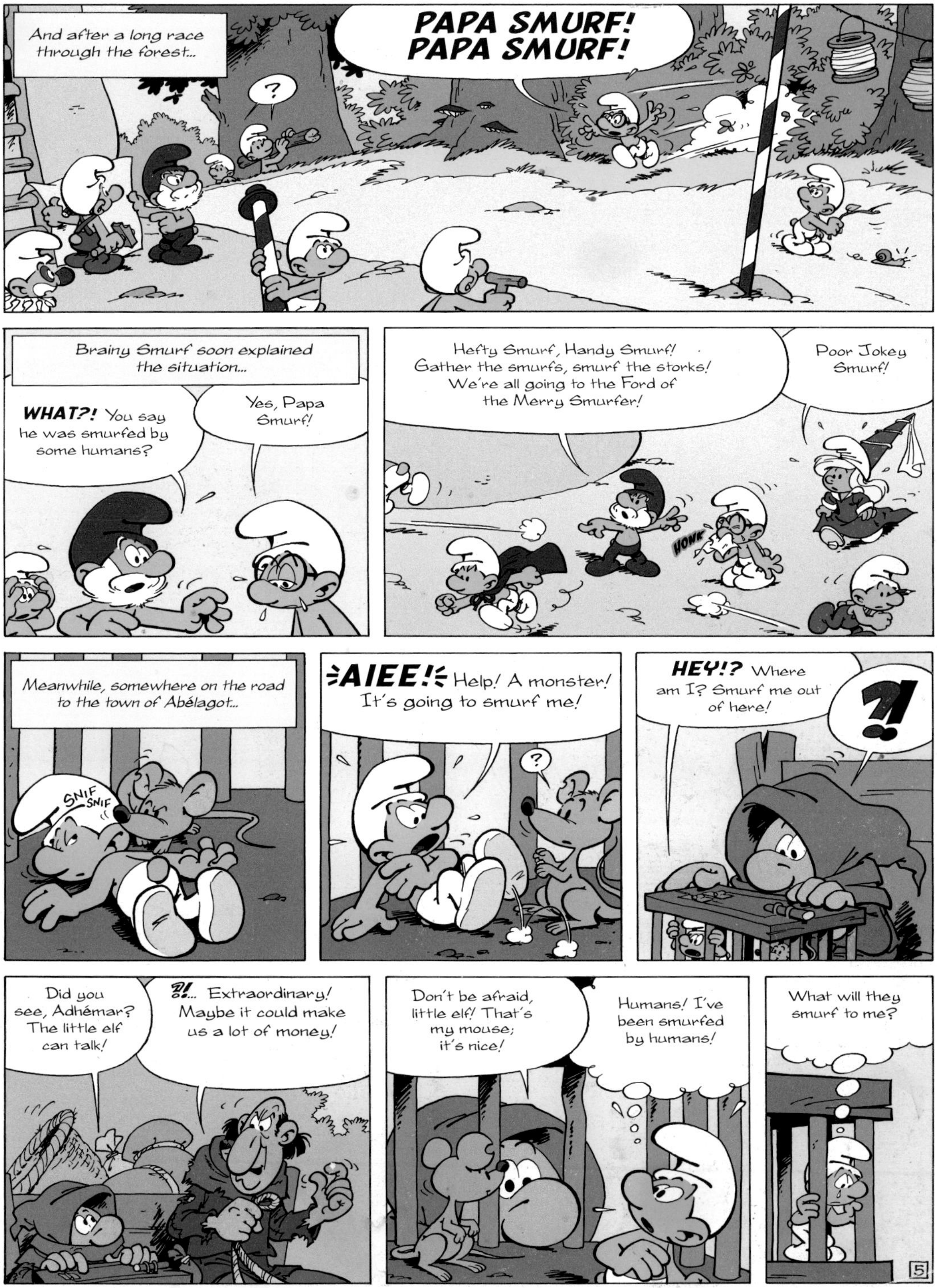

And after a long race through the forest...
PAPA SMURF! PAPA SMURF!
?
Brainy Smurf soon explained the situation...
WHAT?! You say he was smurfed by some humans?
Yes, Papa Smurf!
Hefty Smurf, Handy Smurf! Gather the smurfs, smurf the storks! We're all going to the Ford of the Merry Smurfer!
Poor Jokey Smurf!
HONK
Meanwhile, somewhere on the road to the town of Abélagot...
SNIF SNIF
AIEE! Help! A monster! It's going to smurf me!
?
HEY!? Where am I? Smurf me out of here!
?!
Did you see, Adhémar? The little elf can talk!
?!... Extraordinary! Maybe it could make us a lot of money!
Don't be afraid, little elf! That's my mouse; it's nice!
Humans! I've been smurfed by humans!
What will they smurf to me?
5

You see, Papa Smurf! You can still smurf the imprint of his body!

What do we do, Papa Smurf? Do we catch 'em, bust their smurfs, and free Jokey Smurf?

That wouldn't be very wise, Hefty Smurf! Night will smurf soon! And we don't know whether they went towards Villers or the town of Abélagot!

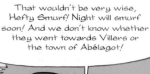

≥Sniff≤

Tomorrow we'll smurf to Homnibus's home! With his crystal ball, he can help us find Jokey Smurf! For now, let's smurf back to the village!

That night, beside the road...

Tomorrow morning, we'll be in the town of Abélagot. Let's hope your mouse won't make us look ridiculous once more!

And you, little elf?! You're not saying anything now! Cootchie cootchie coo... Come on, show us what else you can do!

Stop, Adhémar! Don't bother him!

OWW!

POINK

≥WHAA!≤HA!HA!
Right in his big smurf!

Curthes! A jokethter elf! Thith doethn't bode well!

Hee hee hee!

6

10

The town of Abélagot, the next morning...

HALT!

What's going on, Sergeant?

We must search every vehicle entering and leaving the town!

Search? Why?

Orders are orders! We don't argue!...

Well?

Nothing, Sergeant! They're just street entertainers!

All right! Move along!

That's certainly the first time we've ever been searched at this town's gates. I wonder what's going on?!

They're surely searching for me! Free me, if you don't want to get smurfed, you smurf of thieves!

Hey, gnome, save your breath for when we're at the market! I don't understand anything you say anyhow!

© Peyo

I'm warning you, Godillot, this is your stupid mouse's last chance!

If it blows its number once again--

Don't worry, Adhémar. It'll be fine this time!

Step right up, good people! Come witness an extraordinary show!

?

This mouse originally from a distant land is an unusual animal...

Right before your awe-struck eyes, it will perform a few tricks worthy of the best acrobats!

?

Make way for the most fantastic mouse of all time!

All right, go ahead. Don't be afraid!

8

Heh heh heh!... Now it will do high-flying acrobatics!

It will launch itself from this springboard and perform a triple backflip...

Hup!

And land perfectly... Uh... On... Uh...?!

HA! HA! HA! Ridiculous! And you call that a show?!

Imposters!

BOO! BOO!

Take that! Here's a show for you!

Wait! Don't go— Oww!

Cursed mouse! I warned you!

STOP! SMURF IT ALONE!

?!

You're going about it like nincomsmurfs! Let me out of here, and I'll smurf you how it's done!

Hey?! Did you see that?

What is that thing?

Papa Smurf says you must always smurf animals kindly...

Here!... I brought you an old piece of cheese that was smurfing in the cage!

And now, you'll smurf a little backflip for us!

HUP!

And there! It was no smurfer than that! What do you smurf of that?

What's he saying?

I don't know! I don't understand anything either!

Hmm! I see... I have a tough crowd to deal with!

Good smurfs of Abélagot, you'll smurf the most smurftastic show you've ever smurfed!

Jokey Smurf and the mouse then give a performance that will long remain etched in their memories...

Zeem boom tataaa!...
And that's the show! You can smurf the performers!

BRAVO! BRAVO! FANTASTIC!
CLAP CLAP CLAP CLAP

And now, good people, since performers can't live on love alone, we'll pass among you. Thank you for your generosity...

That little elf is fantastic! And it's barely bigger than a mouse!

!

Look, Godillot! You see all this money? We're rich!

You know you can be even richer?!

?

With this little elf, I can make you a lot of money... More money than you have ever seen!

Let's go to the tavern! We'll be more at ease discussing it over a nice jug of wine!

Uh... Hmm... Godillot, stay here and put the stuff away. I'll be right back!

More money than you've ever seen?!...

It's always the same tune: "Godillot, do this, Godillot, do that!" And of course, **MISTER** Adhémar goes and has a nice drink!

Why don't you dump him?

I can't do that! He's the only one who never makes fun of me for being small!

Small, shmall! I can smurf that one! For me, you'd be a giant instead!

And also, like Papa Smurf says: "However little you may be, you can always find a smurf smaller than you!"

Papa Smurf? Who's that?

He has a big, white beard, red pants, and a red cap. He'll be 543 years old this year at the mushroom harvest, and he's the leader of us Smurfs!

The what? The Smurfs?! And there are many more like you?

There are a hundred of us! And I'm Jokey Smurf!

Hee hee! That doesn't surprise me!

12

There's Adhémar coming back from the tavern! He looks happy!

Well? What did he want from you?

Godillot, thanks to our little friend, we're going to become very, very rich!

?

Meanwhile...

HELLO! Master Omnibus!

NOK NOK

Nobody, Papa Smurf... Not even any sign of Oliver! What do we smurf?

NOK NOK

Hmm... I'm afraid we'll have to smurf for Jokey Smurf ourselves in the world of humans!

GO TO THE WORLD OF HUMANS?!

Me, I don't like the world of humans!

?!

Uh, I'll smurf back to the village to... Uh... Alert the Smurfs!...

YOU'RE COMING WITH US, BRAINY SMURF!

13

17

A moonless night has fallen over Abélagot...

Say, Adhémar, you still haven't explained to me how we'll become rich?!

Your curiosity will soon be satisfied, Godillot! We've arrived at our rendezvous!

You brought the elf?... Perfect! Follow me!

I don't like that smurf there!

Me either!

This is the house of a rich merchant! We'll get started with this one!

?

Let's recap... So, the elf will slip into the house, locate and seize valuables, and bring them back outside to us!

!?

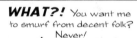

WHAT?! You want me to smurf from decent folk? Never!

The little Smurf is right, Adhémar. We're not crooks!

Come now, Godillot, think! We could get rich a lot faster like that than by being tumblers! And we wouldn't have to tramp along muddy roads anymore!

Keep your voice down! You'll alert the watchmen!

I won't go, in any case. End of discussmurf!

Let me handle it!

14

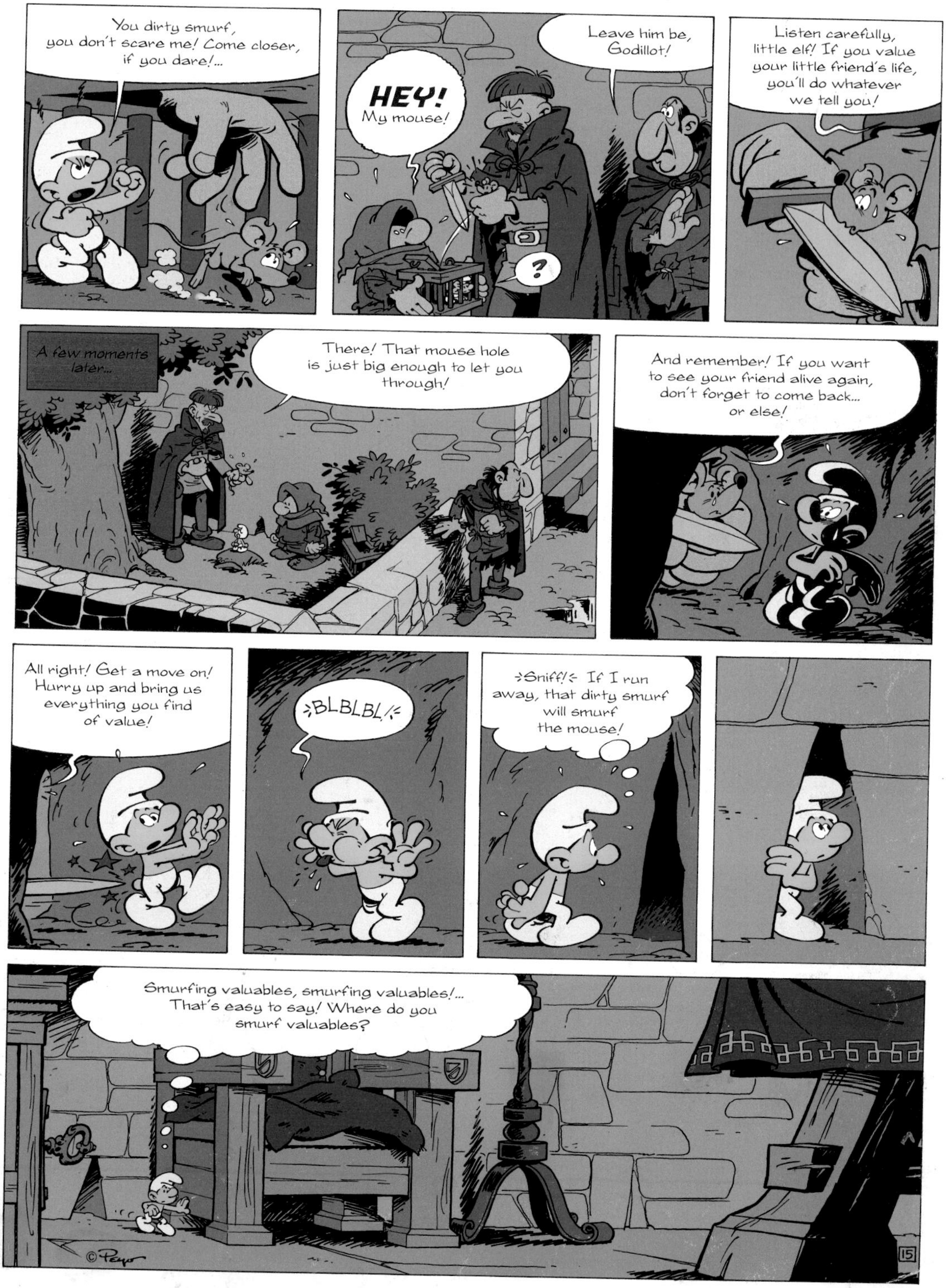

You dirty smurf, you don't scare me! Come closer, if you dare!...
HEY! My mouse!
Leave him be, Godillot!
?
Listen carefully, little elf! If you value your little friend's life, you'll do whatever we tell you!
A few moments later...
There! That mouse hole is just big enough to let you through!
And remember! If you want to see your friend alive again, don't forget to come back... or else!
All right! Get a move on! Hurry up and bring us everything you find of value!
BLBLBL!
Sniff! If I run away, that dirty smurf will smurf the mouse!
Smurfing valuables, smurfing valuables!... That's easy to say! Where do you smurf valuables?
© Peyo
15

Okay, to the left or right?... For smurf's sake! Why don't humans smurf inside mushrooms like everybody else?

Let's see what's smurfing behind this door... ⇒Hmpf⇐!

Yum! The kitchen! Too bad Greedy Smurf isn't here!

?

⇒AAH!⇐

Uh... I-- I... ⇒Gulp!⇐ Nice little kitty... G--go... Sm-- Smurf!

!
ZOOM

By all the smurfs of smurf, it's even bigger than Azrael!

This time, I'm done for! I'm going to get smurfed!

16

BONK

?

BONG

Hee hee! That stupid cat knocked itself out by smurfing that pot off the cabinet.

Maybe you're bigger than Azrael, but you're even stupider than he is! Here, take that, and don't let me catch you here again!

POW

Okay, let's not delay any longer, or else that dirty smurf might smurf the little mouse!

Hup!

Hup!

OH, MY!

In the meantime, outside...

What's keeping him? He's been gone a long time now!

There he is! He's coming back!

!

21

Look what I smurfed you!

But... But what is this?

Well, it's sarsaparilla! Sarsaparilla is good! We Smurfs smurf it all the time!... And there's as much there as you want!

Hee hee hee!

No, you stupid gnome! What we want you to bring us is money, GOLD!

CHOMP CHOMP

CHOMP CHOMP

What? Yum... Gold? Money? ≈Pfff≈ ... That shmurfy shtuff only caushesh problemsh!* And alsho... Yum... Be polite, pleashe!

Get back in there and quick! We must be back at my home before the night watch finds us!

BELCH

Later, the deed is done...

Ten pieces of gold! It's not much!

Pieces of gold are smurfily heavy! It'd be hard for me to smurf more in one trip!

DING DING DILING

And since I only have little pockets, I could smurf only this little shiny stone inside it!

A SHINY STONE ?!

SHOW US!

?

A diamond!

SMURF

Why, of course! Jewels and precious stones aren't heavy... And they're worth lots of money!

⑱

*See THE SMURFS #18 "The Finance Smurf," if you don't believe us!

Listen closely, you wretched blue gnome. Next time, you'll take only stones like this one, understood?

And don't try to escape tonight... Anyways, you don't have anywhere to go! Heh heh heh!

They've made a thief out of me! What would Papa Smurf think, if he saw me?

Will I ever again see The Smurfs?

Meanwhile, a few leagues away, in the sky over Villers...

Do you think Jokey Smurf was smurfed in this city, Papa Smurf?

I don't know, Hefty Smurf! Tomorrow, we'll try to smurf trace of him by inquiring discretely in the village!

We'll smurf the night in this barn!

FLAP FLAP

Smurf yourself a warm, little spot and sleep tight. Tomorrow, we'll have a difficult day!

Goodnight, my little Smurfs!

Goodnight, Papa Smurf!

ZZZ

In the early morn...

COCKADOODLEDOO

?

SCRITCH SCRATCH

ZZZ

AHHH! PP--PAPA SMURF! THERE!... THE SMURF-THING, THERE!

19

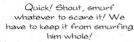

A COW! It has smurfed Grouchy Smurf!

Help! Papa Smuuuuuuuuurf...

Quick! Shout, smurf whatever to scare it! We have to keep it from smurfing him whole!

BOOO!

GRrrrr!

?

Go on! **SHOOO!** Go smurf elsewhere!

MOOOO!

Grouchy Smurf! Are you all right? How do you smurf?

⦂Bleah!⦂ Me, I don't like being smurfed by a cow!

What's going on?! Who could have scared my Marguerite so?

Probably some varmint again!

Quick, Smurfs, let's get out of here!

STOP!

⟨20⟩

24

Smurf yourselves behind this barrel!

Villers' morning market! That smurfs me an idea!

At the market, people always smurf the latest gossip! If Jokey Smurf is in this town, here's where we'll find out about it!

Let's go smurf ourselves among the humans and listen to what they're saying!

Meet back here, around noon!

With courage and discretion, the Smurfs slip into the crowd...

...Attentive to the slightest clue likely to let them find their little, missing friend again...

...and, sometimes, at peril to their lives.

Around noon...

Well? Have any of you smurfed anything interesting?

Wait a moment! Where's Greedy Smurf?

I thought he was with Brainy Smurf!

Ah, no, Papa Smurf! Not at all!... I saw him smurfing with Grumpy Smurf!

Me, I don't like it when-- ?!?

Papa Smurf! LOOK!

GARGAMEL!

He's surely come to smurf us, Papa Smurf! Let's return to the village!

Don't be stupid, Brainy Smurf! He couldn't suspect we're here!

For smurf's sake! If by any chance he stumbles onto Greedy Smurf...

SMACK!

Heh heh! It's kind of nice to be among humans from time to time, far from those cursed Smurfs!

Okay then, let's look at this list! Mandrake roots, three dried frogs, five grams of moondust...

A pound of hazelnuts? Right away, my good lady!

HEY!? What's that thing eating my hazelnuts?

EEEEK!

CRUNCH! NYUMY!

And especially don't forget some soft food for Azrael!

?

EEEEE! There's a blue mouse with a cap eating the hazelnuts!

A little, blue mouse?!... With a cap?... But...

!?

A SMURF! That's a Smurf! Leave him to me. He's mine, all mine!

22

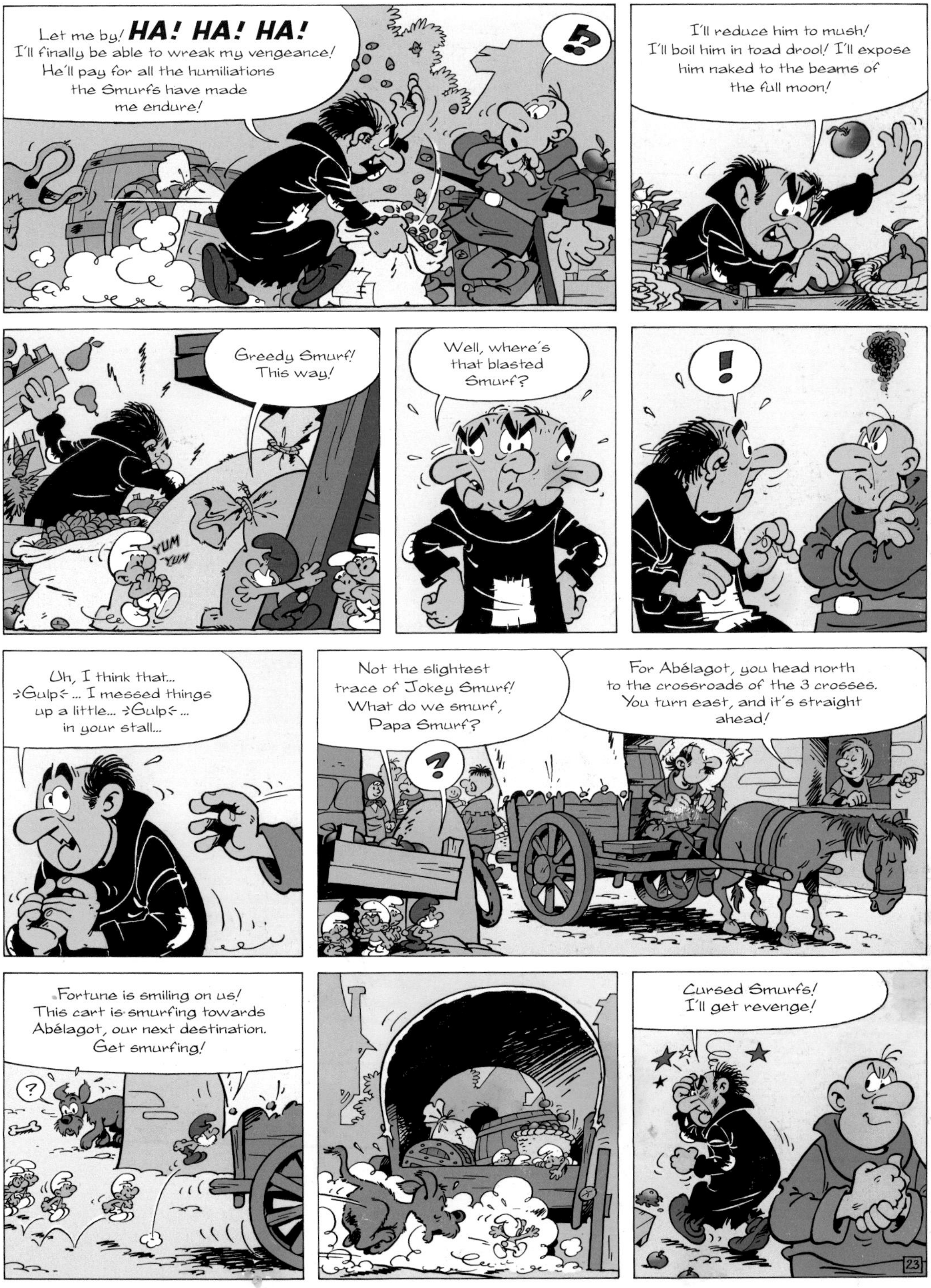
Let me by! HA! HA! HA!
I'll finally be able to wreak my vengeance! He'll pay for all the humiliations the Smurfs have made me endure!
?!
I'll reduce him to mush! I'll boil him in toad drool! I'll expose him naked to the beams of the full moon!
Greedy Smurf! This way!
YUM YUM
Well, where's that blasted Smurf?
!
Uh, I think that... >Gulp<... I messed things up a little... >Gulp<... in your stall...
Not the slightest trace of Jokey Smurf! What do we smurf, Papa Smurf?
?
For Abélagot, you head north to the crossroads of the 3 crosses. You turn east, and it's straight ahead!
Fortune is smiling on us! This cart is smurfing towards Abélagot, our next destination. Get smurfing!
?
Cursed Smurfs! I'll get revenge!
23

That evening, in Abalagot, a new disguise in preparation...

Tonight, we'll go to the herbalist's. In the tavern at noon today, I learned where he hides his jewels.

Here, I sewed you a little disguise which'll make you less visible than with your white pants!

Good idea! Go ahead, Elf, try them on to see!

?

Okay, all right! But turn around. I don't want you seeing my smurf!

Peeping smurfs!

Maybe you should take off your cap, too!

Hee hee hee!

Ah, no! No way! Whoever smurfs my cap, I'll give him a smurf with my hand!

Fine, fine! Okay! Let's go!

Take this sack, you'll be able to carry more jewels at the same time!

And I'll remind you we have our friend in our clutches!

He said: "A chest on the joist over his bed!"

There it is!

Darn! It's smurfed with a lock!

But that won't stop Jokey Smurf! This nail will smurf the trick...

A little skill and...

ABRACADASMURF!

A few instants later...

There, I left a little note to excuse myself. And I left a few jewels! Let's go smurf a look in the other rooms!

ZZZ

OH! Sulphur, coal, everything needed for smurfing a smurf!

Sulphur

Hee hee! That smurfs me a little idea!

I see him. He's coming back, and it was a good haul... His sack is full!

Sapphire rings! Diamond broaches! A pearl necklace! What marvels!

Here, I smurfed a bag especially for you!

For me? That's nice!

BOOM

BLASTED ELF! This time—

Hee hee hee! That was a gift from Jokey Smurf!

Hee hee hee!

Look out! The city watch! Hide!

25

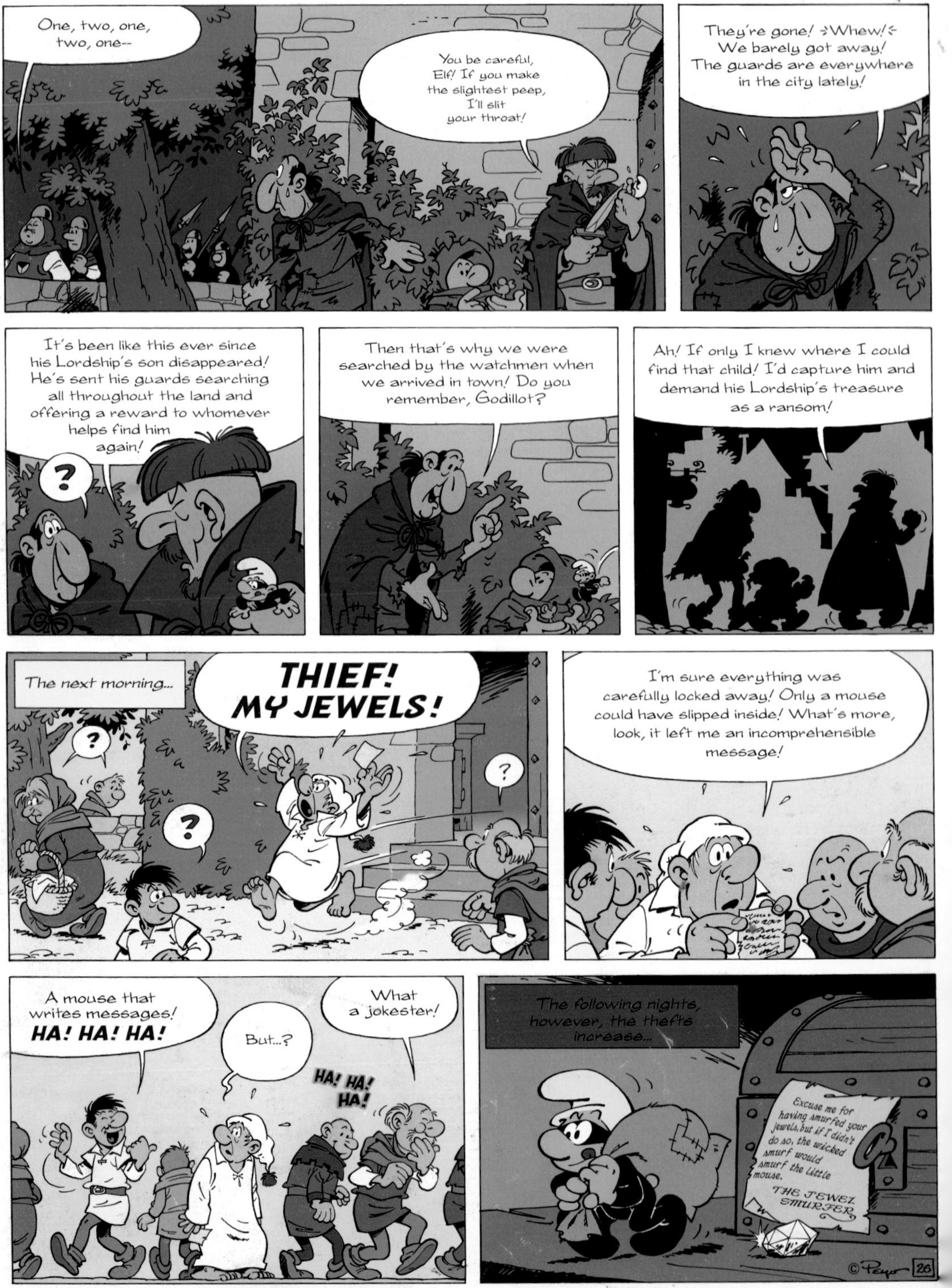
One, two, one, two, one--
You be careful, Elf! If you make the slightest peep, I'll slit your throat!
They're gone! Whew! We barely got away! The guards are everywhere in the city lately!
It's been like this ever since his Lordship's son disappeared! He's sent his guards searching all throughout the land and offering a reward to whomever helps find him again!
?
Then that's why we were searched by the watchmen when we arrived in town! Do you remember, Godillot?
Ah! If only I knew where I could find that child! I'd capture him and demand his Lordship's treasure as a ransom!
The next morning...
THIEF! MY JEWELS!
?
?
?
I'm sure everything was carefully locked away! Only a mouse could have slipped inside! What's more, look, it left me an incomprehensible message!
A mouse that writes messages! HA! HA! HA!
But...?
What a jokester!
HA! HA! HA!
The following nights, however, the thefts increase...
Excuse me for having smurfed your jewels, but if I didn't do so, the wicked smurf would smurf the little mouse.
THE JEWEL SMURFER
© Peyo
26

The villagers must face the facts: a thief is robbing them of their jewels...

?

THE WHITE CROW

Oh, yes, he took everything from me, too!

He left me just one ring and an incomprehensible message! Listen...

"My... Er... Shm-- crmurfest excuses," I don't understand that word! "but it's to sturpf the mouse! If you want to help me, crmurf Papa Shmurp!" What, do you think, is a Papa Shmurp?

?!

Papa Smurf! Papa Smurf!

We've found a trace of Jokey Smurf. He's smurfing all the villagers' jewels!

I know, Hefty Smurf! Everyone's talking about it!

We also know that some jugglers had smurfed an elf in their show! We must find them!... It's surely Jokey Smurf!

That night...

The moneylender is at the tavern. We'll take this chance to steal some of his jewels from him! According to my information, he keeps them hidden in a cupboard in the attic.

Try to bring back as many as possible, since this house is that last one we'll visit in this city! It's getting too dangerous!

!

UH-OH!... ⇒Psst!⇐ ... Adhémar! **THERE!** L-- Look

?!

27

THE MONEYLENDER! HE'S COMING HOME!

Quick, call back the elf!

Too late! He's already in the middle of the room!

Shhhh!

Let's get inside quickly, Milord! It's better not to run into the night watch!

Inside...

With that thief cleaning out the town, the patrols are even more numerous!

?

For Smurf's sake! I'm going to get smurfed!

Holy Moley! What's that?

?

It looks like a little bag.

Strange, indeed!

Bah! It's of no importance! A shot of brandy before we settle down to business, Milord?

♪Whew!♪ ... Luckily, I saw that the door to the cellar wasn't smurfed!

Tonight's a washout! I'll get out through the cellar and resmurf the others!

Oh, my! All the openings are smurfed up! There's no way out through here!

HEY! WHO ARE YOU?

28

NO, WAIT!
I won't do you any harm!
Come back!

⋛Sniff!⋚ Don't leave
me all alone!

⋛BOO HOO HOO!⋚

Why are you
locked up? Were
you bad?

⋛Sniff...⋚

Not at all! My name is
Geoffrey, and I'm the son of
the Lord of this land! I was
abducted by the moneylender
and his accomplice, the traitor
Ganelon, who's pretending to
be my father's friend!

You were
smurfed by wicked
men, too?

They
smurfed me near
my village and
smurfed me
with them!

Now, they're making
me smurf inside houses,
and if I don't do so,
they'll smurf the little
mouse!

What are you
saying? I don't
understand
a thing!

Wait! I'll smurf
you out of that
cage!

?

Hee hee! With
all those nights spent
smurfing, no lock
can resist
me now!

Look out!
Someone's
coming!

33

What's going on? Whom were you talking with?

Uh... W-- Why, with nobody! I wasn't talking!

You were trying to call for help again! Be careful, if you don't want a taste of the lash! In any case, you know full well no one can hear you. All the openings are blocked!

You traitor, when my father learns of your trickery, he'll lock you in his deepest dungeon, where you'll be devoured by rats!

HA! HA! HA!

Don't worry about me, my boy! Before your father learns anything whatsoever, I'll be leagues away from here with the ransom.

⸮Whew!⸮ There you are! We thought you'd been captured!

Let's not stay here!

What's going on? Why do you keep turning back?

I don't know! I have the strange feeling of being followed!

Tomorrow, we'll leave Abélagot. People are getting too distrustful.

30

Later, while everyone is asleep...

That's it! I got it!

If only I could smurf that little piece of wood!

A little hand, Jokey Smurf?

Gladly, Hefty Smurf!

But...

?!

HEFTY SMURF!

Hello, Jokey Smurf! It's been a smurf time since we smurfed each other, don't you think?

Papa Smurf! Grouchy Smurf, Greedy Smurf, and even you, Brainy Smurf! My friends, you all smurfed to my rescue. I'm so happy! But how did you find me?

?

?

...And then we just had to find the tumblers to smurf you! And that's it!

I must admit one thing to you, Papa Smurf! I've smurfed some very wicked things!

Don't worry, Jokey Smurf! I know all about it and I know you have nothing smurfly to blame yourself for!

Before smurfing back to the village, we'll smurf a message to the city watch to report these bandits who forced you to smurf the jewels!

I should also smurf you about a little boy named Geoffrey!

You're not going anywhere except into my sack, you cursed blue elves! HA! HA! HA!

31

35

Godillot! Did you hear that racket? What could it be?

?

What's happening?

What's happening is that tomorrow you can build us a bigger cage because we have five new boarders!

?

The next day...

And there, all done! Now we just have to put it in the cart and we can leave this town!

WE'RE NOT LEAVING NOW!

What? But yesterday, you said...

"Things always look better in the morning," the saying goes!

So, last night, I thought about it and told myself that, with six little elves, we could be more ambitious and seize a treasure that'd make us rich for good! It'd keep us from tramping from town to town!

Yes, but where can we find such a treasure?

I can picture only one place!

AT THE CASTLE!

At-- At the castle? ≥Gulp!≤ You want to rob the Lord?

32

Did you hear, Papa Smurf? He wants to make us smurf a treasure!

36

Exactly, the Lord's treasure! And I have my own idea how to get ourselves into the castle! Godillot, I'll need your talents as a tailor!

?

Later...

HALT! What do you want?

We're entertainers and we'd like to offer our services to the Lord! Our show will surely please him!

IMPOSSIBLE! You mustn't disturb Milord the Duke! He has other things to do besides watching your tomfoolery! Now, go away!

What?!

Guard! Who are those people?

They're just tumblers, Milord Steward. I was going to chase them off, in fact!

One moment! What sort of show are you offering, exactly?

If you'd like to look for yourself, sir!

?

By the king's beard! They're so funny! Where could such things come from?

Ever since the disappearance of his son, Milord the Duke has been rather preoccupied! Tonight, you'll take his mind off it with your show! Come!

33

That evening, just before the show...

Well? Aren't your new costumes lovely?... And try to be convincing this evening, for we must remain a few days in order to scout out the treasure room!...

And to assure myself of your loyalty, I won't keep the mouse any longer...

BUT ONE OF YOU!

You dirty smurf!

HA! HA! HA! This way, I'll be sure you won't get the idea to betray me!

Let Papa Smurf go!

Get ready, tumblers, it'll soon be time to do your tomfoolery!

Shortly after...

Milord the Duke, Fair Lady, Noble Lords, you will be seeing an unprecedented entertainment, hitherto unseen even at the King's court...

These are the elves I told you about, Milord!

Here, coming from a magical land, beings whose existence you've never ever suspected! Here are... THE SMURFS!

34

Let's go, Smurfs, and let's try to smurf 'em a good show!

Me, I don't like smurfing good shows!

I smurf you a very good evening, Milord the Duke! Smurf close attention, for the show is starting!

Greedy Smurf, Brainy Smurf, Jokey Smurf! Smurf the pyramid!

HUP! HUP!

And here's the result!

For your pleasure, here's some smurftastic juggling!

Me, I don't like smurftastic juggling!

Make an effort, Grouchy Smurf! Think of Papa Smurf!

⇎Grmmbl⇎, oh, all right!

YIPPEEE! TRALALAAA! Life is so smurfy!

Why's that one smurfing at me like that? Hasn't he ever seen a Smurf smurfing his zest for life?

For smurf's sake! That's Ganelon, the traitor who smurfed the Duke's son! I forgot to tell Papa Smurf about that!

35

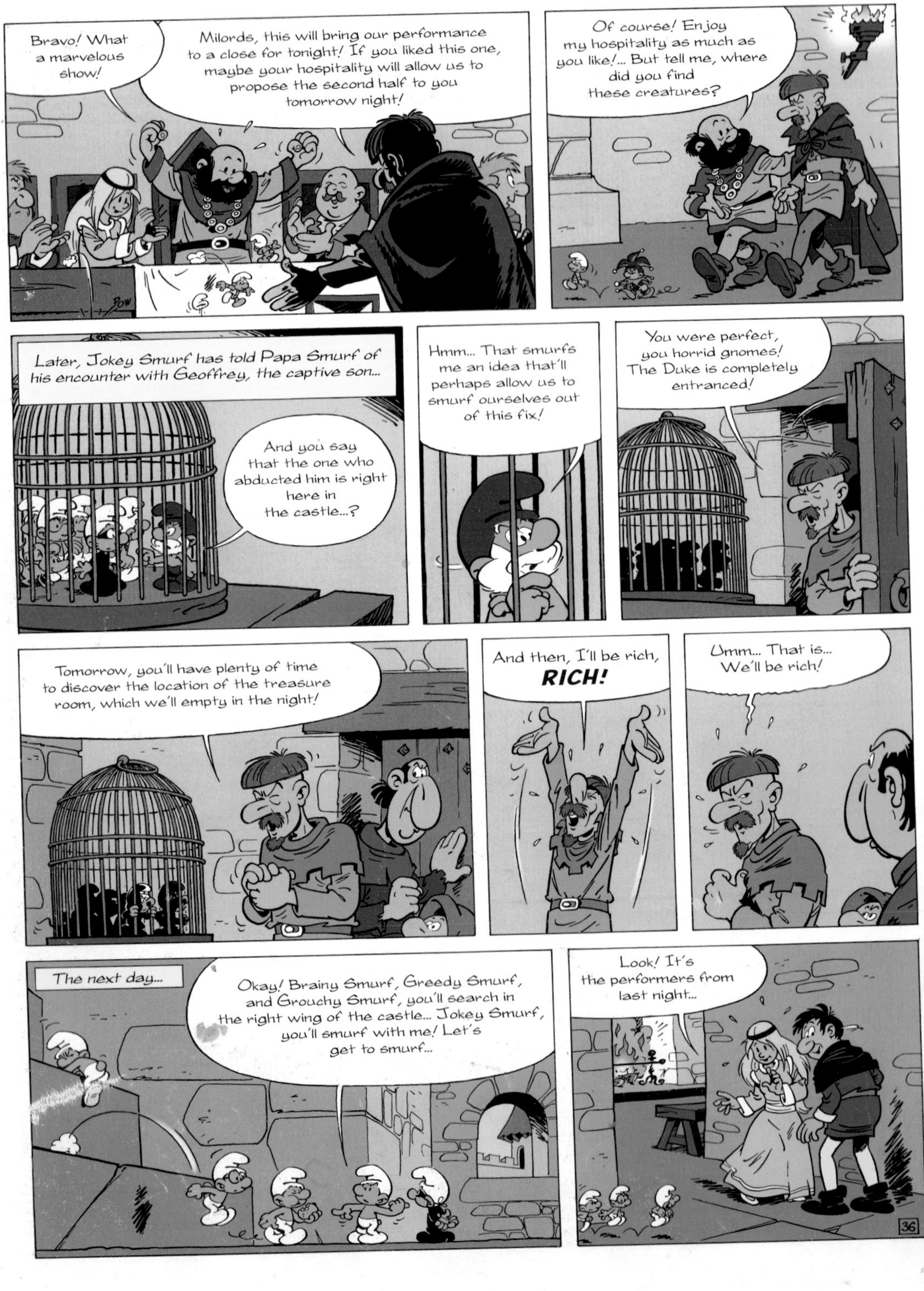
Bravo! What a marvelous show!
Milords, this will bring our performance to a close for tonight! If you liked this one, maybe your hospitality will allow us to propose the second half to you tomorrow night!
POW
Of course! Enjoy my hospitality as much as you like!... But tell me, where did you find these creatures?
Later, Jokey Smurf has told Papa Smurf of his encounter with Geoffrey, the captive son...
And you say that the one who abducted him is right here in the castle...?
Hmm... That smurfs me an idea that'll perhaps allow us to smurf ourselves out of this fix!
You were perfect, you horrid gnomes! The Duke is completely entranced!
Tomorrow, you'll have plenty of time to discover the location of the treasure room, which we'll empty in the night!
And then, I'll be rich, RICH!
Umm... That is... We'll be rich!
The next day...
Okay! Brainy Smurf, Greedy Smurf, and Grouchy Smurf, you'll search in the right wing of the castle... Jokey Smurf, you'll smurf with me! Let's get to smurf...
Look! It's the performers from last night...
36

I don't understand why we must smurf for the treasure room if Papa Smurf has a plan to smurf us out of here without stealing the treasure...

It's to lull our abductors' distrust, Grouchy Smurf!... What's more, Papa Smurf asked us to smurf a few things for this evening's performance!

Not here! Those are the kitchens! Let's smurf that way!

Me, I don't like the kitchens!

?

AH! Here's the laundry room! Rags and sponges... With that, we'll be able to smurf the costumes!

Here! Smurf at this, Greedy Smurf!

?

What?! Where did Greedy Smurf go?

INCREDIBLE! Where can he put all that?

YUM
CHOMP
SLURP
CRUNCH
GULP
YUM

In the other wing of the castle...

We won't smurf anything over this way, Jokey Smurf! Let's rejoin the others!

Tell me, Hefty Smurf, we surely can smurf an herbalist in this castle, don't you think?

?

It'd just be to smurf some sulphur, a little bit of coal, and few other smurferies!

I can guess your intentions, Jokey Smurf! You are truly incorrigible!

Help me smurf it! It's for a little surprise!

© Peyo

37

Meanwhile, Papa Smurf attempts to make himself an ally...

You think so, Milord Papa Smurf? Yes... Perhaps!

Papa Smurf, we've smurfed everything you asked us for!

Well done, my little Smurfs!

Good! Does everyone know what he must smurf this evening?

Yes, Papa Smurf!

Ah! You're back! Did you find the treasure room?

No, becau—

POW

Uh... Yes, **YES!** It's smurfed uh... in the castle's south wing! It's not smurfed by a guard! That's it! Heh heh heh!

OUGH

Perfect! We'll get to work tonight, after your show!

And that evening...

Ah! At last! Here are the artists!

Noble Lord, we're going to smurf you a small theatrical smurf that will be smurfed by my companions here present, and which will be narrated to you by your servant, myself, in person... Which is, moreover, ensmurfly normal, for having a more satismurfery diction, I was the only one who...

!

OKAY! OKAY! Everyone has understood, Brainy Smurf! Let's begin!

Uh... All right, Hefty Smurf!

Hum... *Hear the sad tale of two smurfducted beings, far from their families...*

38

42

≁Pff≁... A sad tale! I preferred it when it was tumbling!

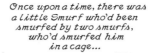

Once upon a time, there was a little Smurf who'd been smurfed by two smurfs, who'd smurfed him in a cage...

≁Sniff!≁ What will they smurf to me?

At first, they displayed him along with a mouse that shared his plight...

Soon, however, an ill-intentioned fellow made his appearance...

Me, I don't like being the ill-intentioned fellow!

What?! That's me! Would they betray me? No! It's not possible. They wouldn't dare! Their leader is my hostage!

In the meantime, Papa Smurf continues his persuasive attempts...

...The poor Smurf was forced to smurf by night into the homes of honest smurfs, and to smurf their jewels therein...

Which sowed discord amongst the populasmurf...

Tell me, steward. Doesn't this remind you of something?... Haven't the town folk been complaining about mysterious thefts of late?

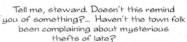

Indeed, Milord! It does ring a bell...

Say, you two! If I'm bothering you, you must smurf so!

If you start again, I'll tell Papa Smurf, for Papa Smurf always says you mustn't smurf a word while someone else is talking!

Okay! Let's smurf again! *Back to our story... After fleecing the populasmurf, the thieves decided to smurf the Lord's treasure...*

39

The cursed gnomes! I must do something!

The latter, a generous duke, beloved by all his smurfs, was languishing in despair.

SIGH!

Did you see, Milord Duke?! That's the spitting image of you!

His sadness was great, for his young son had disappeared, and no one knew what had become of him... ≽Sniff!≼

O smurf, o despair...

HONK

What he didn't know was that his son, for whom he wept, had been smurfed by a smurf pretending to be his friend!

?!

Heh heh heh!

SPPRRITTZZ

THAT'S ENOUGH! This story isn't amusing me at all!

?

!

You, tumbler! What does all this mean? And you, Ganelon? Why does that elf resemble you? I want explanations!

Milord, this-- this is an affront to our friendship! This is all purely an invention!

Umm... Absolutely, Milord! These elves are highly imaginative... It-- it's nothing but theater!

THAT'S A LIE!

40

?

?

?

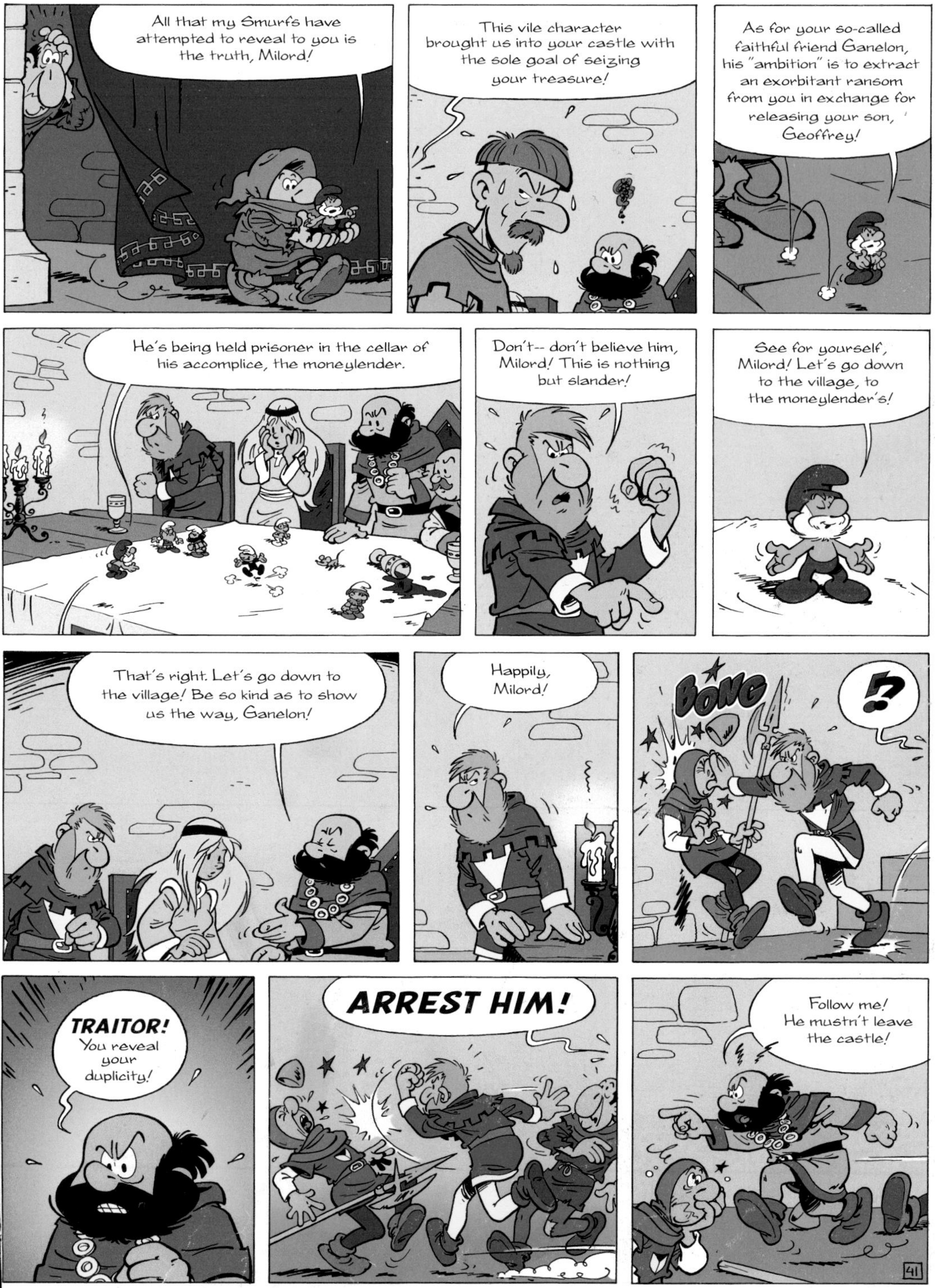

All that my Smurfs have attempted to reveal to you is the truth, Milord!
This vile character brought us into your castle with the sole goal of seizing your treasure!
As for your so-called faithful friend Ganelon, his "ambition" is to extract an exorbitant ransom from you in exchange for releasing your son, Geoffrey!
He's being held prisoner in the cellar of his accomplice, the moneylender.
Don't-- don't believe him, Milord! This is nothing but slander!
See for yourself, Milord! Let's go down to the village, to the moneylender's!
That's right. Let's go down to the village! Be so kind as to show us the way, Ganelon!
Happily, Milord!
BONG
!?
TRAITOR! You reveal your duplicity!
ARREST HIM!
Follow me! He mustn't leave the castle!
41

All the guards are pursuing the traitor, Ganelon! They've completely forgotten me!

All the guards?!... Heh heh! But by all the demons of darkness, that gives me an idea!

YIPPEEEE! Hurray for Papa Smurf!

I'm proud of you, my little Smurfs! Thanks to you, this matter is finally concluded!

THAT'S WHAT YOU THINK!

Are you still here? Clearly you're a stubborn one!

More than you think, elf! You're going to lead me to the treasure room! And quick!

As for you two, the gnome's treachery means our deal is off! I'm keeping the treasure for myself! And don't try to follow us, or else...

Meanwhile, Ganelon is on the run...

If I can reach the stables, I can escape through the northern gate! It's surely not guarded!

OOPS! Change of plans!

THERE HE IS! CAPTURE HIM!

On the other side of the castle...

Are you sure it's this way?

© Peyo

42

What now? Which way do we go?

Uh... this way!

HEY! Wait for me!

He mustn't smurf that we don't know where the treasure room is located! Let's lead him into the castle...

And meanwhile, Ganelon is fleeing...

The south tower and its secret passage! It's my last chance!

⇒Pff⇐... Don't go so fast!

⇒Huff⇐... ⇒Puff⇐... I've earned this treasure!

Hey, is it far away yet?

No, no! Not that much!

And in the meantime...

Victory! After this corner, it's...

?

P·OW

Ah ha! Two birds with one stone! Capture them and lock them in the tower!

?

43

A few moments later, it's the two crooks' turn to discover the joys of life behind bars...

In the castle and throughout the land the reunion of the Duke and his son Geoffrey lead to festivities that lasted for days...

For having repented, Godillot became the Duke's protégé and was even able to choose a servant whose pardon he'd obtained...

A few days later, the moment for farewells arrived...

Tell me, Jokey Smurf, what did you smurf with all the ingredients that you smurfed in the castle?

Hee hee hee! I made presents out of it, and I asked a guard to smurf them to our "friends" in their cells!

BOOM
BOOM

HA! HA! HA! HA!
HA!

As for the great festival of the spring equinox, despite the absence of the cattail stalks, it was a true success!

Tell me, Greedy Smurf... Besides eating, did you smurf anything useful in all this?

?

YUM
YUM SLURP

END